I, MARKED

JT BALDWIN

"The subject's previous identity must be completely dissolved before reconstruction can begin. Emotional attachments, personal history, and individual preferences represent structural weaknesses that compromise operational efficiency. Only through systematic elimination of these elements can we achieve the precision required for institutional service."

— From "Enhancement Protocols, Third Edition" by Dr. Evelyn Baeriss

Series Guide | THE PALISADE JOURNALS

RECOMMENDED READING ORDER:

Vol. I — The Thermecine Road (2178)
Vol. II — Chief Minister (2191)
Vol. III — I, Marked (2173)
Vol. IV — Test of Character (2183)
Vol. V — Fortune Forged (2189)

CHRONOLOGICAL TIMELINE:

▸ **2173 | *I, Marked* ◂ You Are Here**
A girl named Anne becomes a weapon called Snips.

• 2178 | *The Thermecine Road*
Regal Eldain begins his descent down the road of vengeance.

• 2183 | *Test of Character*
Victoria Colwell witnesses an unspeakable transfer of power.

• 2189 | *Fortune Forged*
Peri Blackwood's first con and the cost of leadership.

• 2191 | *Chief Minister*
The highest office is not enough for Shori Ashford.

PART ONE

THE COURIER

Late Autumn, 2173
Rosemont District, East of Beltmoire, Continental Authority

Anne Calder stepped off the Union rail carriage with her courier bag cutting into her shoulder and a job in her pocket that could erase her debts or end her. She hadn't decided which was more likely.

Rosemont Station smelled like salt air and coal smoke and the sweet citrus coming off the vendor carts near the plaza. Heat rippled off the polished stone pathway. A carefully maintained front door on a city that was rotting from the inside.

For the first time in weeks, she could breathe without tasting factory disinfectant.

She stretched her legs, jacket tied at her waist, tank top sticking in the humid air. Her dark brown hair hung in a loose twist that swayed as she turned to take in the station. Just over five feet tall, and her mother's voice somewhere behind everything: *You see people as they truly are when they think you're beneath them.*

Two Wardens stood near the main information board. Dark blue uniforms, crisp despite the heat. The first one helped an elderly woman find her platform, patient, respectful. Normal.

The second one was wrong.

Anne watched him check his brass pocket watch and scan the crowd. Too methodical. Too focused. The way he tracked faces wasn't keeping the peace. It was hunting. And when he spoke to his partner, she caught a fragment of accent that didn't match the uniform. She'd heard inflections like that in Beltmoire's back alleys, on men who wore borrowed clothes and carried debts they couldn't pay down.

Probably nothing. But probably nothing had kept her alive for three years.

A young mother was struggling nearby. Two oversized bags, a crying toddler, and the particular exhaustion of someone who'd been managing alone for too long.

Anne grabbed one of the bags without asking. "Platform six, right? I saw it on the board."

The woman looked up. "Thank you, dear. The 4:30 to Solstice Bay. I'm meeting my grandbabies."

"Third car back has the family section. More space for bags, better seats." Anne adjusted her pace for the tired child. "They'll be glad to see you."

"You're very kind."

The word caught somewhere under Anne's ribs. She didn't argue with it. Just handed back the bag at the platform entrance and watched the woman disappear into the crowd.

"ATTENTION PASSENGERS: THE WESTERN EXPRESS TO HAMMISON WILL DEPART FROM PLATFORM SEVEN IN

FIFTEEN MINUTES. ALL PASSENGERS SHOULD PROCEED TO PLATFORM SEVEN FOR BOARDING."

The announcement detonated directly above her head. Anne ducked, hands flying to her ears, heart slamming before her brain caught up with the fact that nobody was shooting at her.

"Swear they built these things to rupture eardrums," she muttered, rubbing her ear. Around her, other travelers were recovering from the same assault with varying degrees of dignity.

She adjusted her courier bag and felt the slip of paper with Hull's name crinkle in her pocket. Three years of running packages had taught her when a job felt heavier than the bag. Hull wasn't just any client. His name carried whispers in courier circles. Government work that paid enough to clear serious debt, the kind that left marks on people who took it.

Time to get back to work.

The glass doors opened with a soft hiss, and she stepped out into Beltmoire proper.

The change was immediate.

The polished facade of Rosemont fell away like a stage set struck between acts. Beyond the terminal district, the city showed its real face. Paint peeling from buildings in long strips. Storefronts boarded up or cracked in spider-web patterns. Cobblestones shifting under every step, settling into the particular geometry of a place that had been sinking for decades.

But the sounds were what got her. Beltmoire creaked. Wooden supports groaned in buildings that had stood for over a century. Metal expansion joints in the elevated rail lines clicked and popped as they cooled in the late afternoon air.

The city was dying, but it refused to die.

An old man on a corner stool repaired shoes with tools older than the Continental Authority. He nodded as she passed. *I see you, fellow survivor.* A few blocks further, a violin drifted from an open window. More heart than skill, the melody wandering through folk tunes that had probably been old when Beltmoire was young.

Anne walked west, following the address.

The checkpoint appeared where the courier network said it would. A government building at the edge of the district, the kind of place that existed on official maps but not in conversation. Anne went through the front entrance like a legitimate courier, because she was one, and presented her papers with the casual confidence of someone who'd never been caught at anything she'd actually been doing.

The security guard looked surprised. "Not every day I get to see someone like you with proper papers. Aren't you supposed to be sneaking in?"

"Yeah, but then I'd miss that look and this conversation." She hefted her courier bag. "Besides, I've got legit work today."

"Fine. Who are you here to see?"

Anne reached into her bag and handed over the slip of paper. One word: *Hull.*

The guard's expression changed. Something tightened around his eyes, the way it does when a person handles a name that weighs more than they're comfortable lifting. "Sensitive cargo, huh?" He keyed his mic. "Gate Bravo Seven to SecBase. Civilian at perimeter requesting Commander Hull."

A pause. Then he added, "Girl with an attitude."

Anne's eyebrows shot up. *Really?* But she held her tongue. The guard listened to his earpiece, nodded.

"Transport inbound for pickup."

Thirty seconds later, a dark vehicle pulled into view. Windows tinted. Engine idling. No markings, no insignia, no hint of where it was going or what it was for.

Three years of dirty jobs, late-night runs, and reputation-building had brought her to this moment. A job that might finally clear her debts and buy her a way out.

Her hand trembled against the strap of her courier bag. She made it stop.

She climbed in.

I, Marked

PART TWO

THE CROSSING

Late Autumn, 2173

Abandoned Airfield (B.E. Langley), Northern Military Zone, CA

The transport wheezed to a stop at the checkpoint with the mechanical sigh of something that had seen better decades. Anne shouldered her courier bag and stepped into the salty air, boots hitting gravel with the confidence of someone who'd never missed a delivery. Even when she was running fifteen minutes behind.

The convoy waited ahead. Three black vehicles, engines idling, official plates catching the muted running lights. Men in tactical gear checked weapons and studied maps.

Anne took one look at the setup and shook her head. "Two escort vehicles, huh? Going for that 'nothing to see here' vibe?"

A laugh rough as gravel came from behind her. "Subtle ain't exactly our strong suit."

She turned. Grizzled. Medical corps insignia. Scars mapping old violence across a face that had stopped being surprised by anything a long time ago. Taegus Hull, according to her briefing notes. A soldier who'd survived by being better at killing than dying.

"You're late," he said. No heat. Just observation.

"Traffic in Beltmoire." True enough, if you didn't count the grandmother at the station. "But I'm here, and your cargo gets delivered on schedule. That's what you pay me for."

Hull's expression shifted. "UAD Beltmoire? You mean..."

"Beltmoire ain't Union, you best remember that." Sharp. The kind of edge that said this wasn't her first time. "The mob runs that town, and they don't much care what your official maps say. You want to drive through there flashing CA tags and talking about Union Administrative Districts, you do it without me."

"Fair enough." His eyes recalculated. "Last I checked, we're standing in Continental Authority territory. And you got yourself contracted to soldiers. Different rules."

"Different rules, same bullshit." She gestured toward the convoy. "What's the real story here? Nobody sends three vehicles and a full security detail for a routine courier run."

Hull studied her. Deciding something. "How old are you, twelve? Do you even know how to drive?"

"Who recommended me?" Anne shot back. "You should ask them."

His laugh was dry as dust. "Fair point. Package is high-value. Sensitive cargo that needs discreet handling."

"Discreet? This firepower is way past discreet. You're advertising trouble."

"Sometimes trouble's the best deterrent." He gestured toward the lead vehicle.

"So what's worth all this?"

His expression closed down. "Curious little thing, aren't you?"

"I'm the courier. I need to know what I'm carrying, what kind of heat it might bring, and who might try to take it from me." Level. Professional. "It's not curiosity, it's survival."

"Eight-year-old girl, sedated for transport." Hull's voice carried something that hadn't been there before. Not guilt. Proximity to it. "Eyes that make her valuable to certain people. People who don't take no for an answer. Or like it when twelve-year-old couriers ask too many questions."

"Hells, I'm seventeen." But something cold was settling in her stomach. She'd heard whispers. Kids born different. Taken for things the Authority didn't put in writing. "What happens to her?"

"That's need-to-know."

"The hell it is." Harder than she'd intended. "I don't transport kids to places where bad things happen to them. That's not courier work, that's..."

"It's the job." Hull's voice cut clean. "And if you can't handle it, we'll find someone who can."

Anne looked at his face. Read it the way she'd been reading faces since she was old enough to understand that adults lied with their mouths but told the truth with everything else. Hull wasn't cruel. He was compliant. A man who'd drawn a line between following orders and asking what the orders meant, and he'd drawn it so long ago he'd forgotten it was a choice.

She'd pushed too far. "Yeah, yeah, yeah. I don't care what you do. I was just making small talk. I get paid to escort, not for conversation."

Hull studied her. The flat expression of someone who'd heard that kind of backpedal before. The silence sat between them.

"Where are we taking her?" Anne asked.

"UAD Port Franklin. Medical wellness facility for evaluation and processing."

"Reed's Harbor." She knew the place. Officially UAD Port Franklin, but nobody called it that except government clerks and people trying to impress tourists. "That's smuggler's territory."

"That's Continental Authority territory. And it's where the job takes us."

She looked at the convoy again. The tactical gear wasn't for show. These men moved with the loose readiness of recent combat. The vehicles were armored, government issue, modified for serious opposition.

"How many people want this kid?" she asked.

"Enough that we're taking the scenic route and moving fast." Hull started toward the lead vehicle. "You ride with me. If we make it to the extraction point, the boss'll handle the rest."

The way he said *the boss*. Respect and something else. Something that made a career soldier choose his words carefully.

"Contingency plans?"

"What we do when someone tries to take our cargo."

Not if. When.

"All right." She shouldered her bag. "Let's get this over with."

As they walked toward the vehicles, Anne let herself look.

The middle car. Tinted windows. She could make out the shape through the glass. Small. Head lolled against the seat restraint, the unnatural stillness of chemical sedation. Eight years old. A child strapped into the back of an armored vehicle like munitions being transferred between depots.

She told herself the job was simple. Transport a package from point A to point B. Everything else was someone else's problem.

Her stomach didn't believe her.

She climbed into the lead vehicle.

⟡

The convoy pulled out under cover of darkness, three black vehicles heading north along the coastal highway toward Reed's Harbor.

Anne settled into the passenger seat and tried to find a comfortable way to sit in a vehicle that had been designed for soldiers, not seventeen-year-old girls with courier bags. The seat was too wide. The dash too far away. The whole interior smelled like gun oil and government soap, and the windows turned everything outside into tinted amber.

She'd never seen the world from inside something this clean.

Hull drove the first stretch in silence. Eyes flicking from the road to his mirrors and back. The occasional streetlight threw pale stripes across the dashboard, and Anne watched them wash across his face. Light, dark. Light, dark. Like a clock counting off something she couldn't see.

They passed through the edge of Beltmoire heading north. The covered market at Sable Crossing. The elevated rail trestle where pigeons nested in the ironwork. The Cannery District, where the Andori crews loaded trucks in broad daylight because nobody with a badge felt like dying over it.

She catalogued the route. Left on Meridian. Right on Harborline, where the road curved and the buildings thinned and the salt air got stronger. Courier habit. If she had to walk back, she wanted to know the distance.

The city was thinning. Fewer lights. Fewer people.

They passed Greer Street.

Anne looked away from the window.

She looked back. The building was already gone. Just a flash. A brick front with a fire escape that leaned two degrees off plumb. Third floor. The window with the towel stuffed in the crack because the landlord never fixed the draft.

Lena's window.

It came up fast. Not a memory she chose.

The stairwell. The smell first. Sweet and chemical and wrong. Anne had taken the stairs two at a time because Lena hadn't answered the door in three days and the neighbors had stopped knocking.

The door was unlocked.

Lena was on the bathroom floor. Not unconscious. Worse. Awake. Eyes open, staring at the ceiling with the particular emptiness of someone who'd stopped fighting and hadn't told anyone. A glass pipe on the tile. Burn marks on her fingertips. The room smelled like a place where something had died, and the thing that had died was her sister's willingness to keep going.

Anne had gotten on her knees. Right there on the tile, in whatever was on that floor.

"Get up." Her voice cracking. Fifteen years old. "Lena. Get up. You can't do this."

Lena's eyes found her. Focused, barely. The way a signal fades before the station goes dark.

"It's easier down here, Annie."

"I don't care. Get up."

"You will." Lena's hand came up and touched her cheek. Gentle. The ghost of the sister who used to walk her to school and check under the bed and split the last bread roll so Anne got the bigger half. "You will care. When you see what it's like. How heavy everything gets. You'll understand why the floor feels better than standing."

Anne pulled at her. Tried to lift her. Lena weighed nothing and everything.

"Please."

"Go home, Annie."

"You're my home."

Lena closed her eyes. Done. The conversation over because she'd decided it was, and nothing Anne could do with her hands or her voice or her fifteen years of not knowing how the world worked could change the physics of a person who'd stopped wanting to stand.

Anne stayed on that floor until her knees went numb. Then she got up, because someone had to, and walked down three flights of stairs and out into Beltmoire.

She never saw Lena alive again.

The vehicle hit a bump in the road. Anne's hand found her courier bag and pressed against the hard edges inside it.

Beltmoire was gone behind them. The road ahead was dark.

She didn't think about bathroom floors.

⚙

Hull broke the silence somewhere past the city limits.

"Ever patch a gut wound in the middle of a firefight with nothing but gauze, fishing line, and a bottle of grain alcohol?"

Anne glanced at him. "No, but I did sew a radiator shut with copper wire in the middle of a thunderstorm once."

"Bet the radiator didn't scream at you."

"No." Dryly. "But the mechanic did."

Hull chuckled, then winced. "Remind me not to laugh."

Moonlight flashed off the cliffside walls as the highway wound north. The Marks opened up below them to the right. An exclusive stretch of beachfront estates where wealth bought silence, privacy, and armed response times under sixty seconds. Massive houses blazing with light on landscaped slopes. The kind of wealth that insulated people from knowing what their government moved along the roads above them in the dark.

Anne shifted in her seat. The convoy behind them was visible in the side mirror. Running lights, steady interval, the second vehicle maintaining distance.

The girl was in that vehicle.

"She woke up once," Hull said. Not looking at her. Eyes on the road. "During the transfer at the airfield. Sedation was wearing off. Had to re-dose her."

Anne didn't say anything.

"Her eyes opened for maybe ten seconds." Hull's hands adjusted on the wheel. "Kid looked right at me. Didn't cry. Didn't scream. Just... looked."

Something in his voice had changed. The professional flatness had cracked, just slightly, the way concrete cracks when the ground shifts underneath it.

Anne didn't ask anything else. Hull didn't offer.

✧

The convoy stopped at a fuel point. A dead service station off the highway, no lights, the pumps rigged for military vehicles. Hull's men moved with practiced efficiency, checking tires, checking weapons, the quick business of a team that knew the clock was running.

Anne got out to stretch her legs. The cold hit immediately. She pulled her jacket tighter and walked the perimeter the way a courier walked any unfamiliar stop: exits, sightlines, the distance to the tree line if things went wrong.

She passed the middle vehicle.

The rear door was open. One of Hull's men was checking the girl's IV, adjusting the drip with the mechanical attention of someone performing a task he didn't want to think about too carefully. He stepped back and moved toward the fuel pumps.

Anne looked at the girl.

Small. Smaller than eight should be. Long dark braids against mahogany skin. Her chest rose and fell with the shallow rhythm of chemical sleep. Her hands were curled at her sides, fingers loose, palms up. The posture of total surrender. A body that had been placed here by other hands and had no say in where it went next.

Then the girl's face shifted. A flinch, or a dream. Her eyes opened for a moment, unfocused, not seeing anything. Anne caught the color before they closed again. Not brown. Amber, maybe. Something about it she couldn't place.

She stepped back from the vehicle and walked to the lead car.

Hull was already behind the wheel, engine running. She pulled the door shut and settled into the passenger seat. The convoy rolled back onto the highway in formation. Running lights in the mirror. The dark road ahead.

They drove in silence for a while. The Marks were closer now, the estate lights brighter through the trees, the road curving along the coast where the cliffs dropped toward the water. Anne watched the treeline and tried not to think about the girl in the vehicle behind them. The small hands. The palms turned up.

Hull checked his mirrors. "Twenty minutes to the extraction point. Scenic route, like I said."

"Scenic." Anne looked at the mansions glowing through the trees. "Sure."

The road straightened. Hull's shoulders had just started to ease off the wheel when the night split open.

The explosion hit the road ahead of them. Not sound first. Light. A white flash that seared Anne's vision and turned the windshield into a wall of brightness, and then the sound arrived and it was everywhere, inside the vehicle, inside her chest, a concussion that rattled her teeth and shoved the air out of her lungs.

Hull's hands were already moving. Wheel jerking left. Brakes. But momentum was a physics problem that reflexes couldn't solve, and the vehicle slid forward into the debris field. Something hit the hood. Something else cracked the windshield on Anne's side, a spider-web fracture that appeared without warning three inches from her face.

Behind them, gunfire. The treeline lighting up with muzzle flashes, strobing in the dark, the sound arriving in bursts that overlapped into a continuous roar.

"Contact rear!" The radio. "Multiple hostiles, both flanks!"

Hull shoved his door open and half-fell out. Blood was already blooming across his sleeve. Shrapnel. He hadn't even registered it. "Return fire! Secure the package!"

Anne was in the driver's seat before she'd made a conscious decision to move. Her hands found the wheel and the gearshift and the accelerator and all of it was automatic, all of it was muscle memory from three years of running packages through Beltmoire's worst streets at speeds that turned corners into coin flips.

"What the hell are you doing?" Hull barked.

"Getting us out of this kill zone." She gunned the engine. "You want to sit here and get shot, or you want to live long enough to deliver your package?"

Hull came around the front, keeping low. Bullets sparked off the hood. He dove into the passenger seat, grimacing as he braced his rifle against the door frame. "Drive."

She floored it.

The access road was narrow. Estate walls on both sides, close enough that the side mirrors were a liability. Anne took the first corner blind and felt the vehicle's weight shift, the rear end swinging wide, tires screaming on pavement that had been designed for Sunday drives at twenty miles an hour. The steering wheel fought her. She fought back. The vehicle straightened.

Behind them, the second convoy vehicle followed. Its driver was smart enough to stick with someone who clearly knew what she was doing, or too scared to try anything else.

"This isn't the route," Hull said, firing controlled bursts out the window.

"Your route got us ambushed." Another corner. Tighter. She felt the wheel shudder and held it through the turn by grip and instinct. "I'm improvising."

The Marks at night was a maze of winding roads, mansion gates, manicured hedges that blocked sightlines. Anne used all of it. She cut through estate driveways and looped back through service roads and took a straightaway fast enough to press Hull against his seat. The pursuit vehicles behind them were bigger, heavier, built for open road. On these narrow curves, that size was a prison.

Hull fired again. The recoil vibrated through the vehicle.

"Where are you taking us?" he demanded.

"Beach access. We lose the wheels, find alternative transport."

The road dropped toward the coast. Sand dunes. Scattered debris. Old construction materials, discarded pier sections, the detritus of coastal development. Anne threaded between obstacles by moonlight and memory and the particular instinct of someone who'd been navigating bad terrain since she was old enough to run.

The engine coughed.

Wheels spinning. Sand in the undercarriage. The vehicle shuddered and dug itself in and stopped.

"Shit," Anne said.

"Now what?" Hull's face was gray in the dashboard light.

She looked ahead. Expensive boats bobbed at private docks, their lights reflecting off dark water. "Now we improvise."

They abandoned the vehicles on the sand. Hull's men transferred the girl with the efficiency of people who'd practiced the handoff. Anne caught a glimpse of her as they carried her toward the water. Long dark braids. Mahogany skin. The stillness of a body that had no say in its own direction.

Anne focused on the boats.

"This'll do." She was already working the ignition system. "Owner's probably having dinner somewhere, telling his friends about his latest acquisition."

Hull watched her bypass the security. "Where'd you learn that?"

"Beltmoire waterfront. Folks like you frown at this." The engine caught. "All aboard our borrowed ride."

The boat responded clean. Smooth acceleration, tight steering. Anne set bearings north and pushed the throttle forward. The Marks fell away on both sides, massive houses blazing with light, floor-to-ceiling windows showing dinner parties and evening gatherings. People in expensive clothes holding expensive glasses, living expensive lives on a coastline where a stolen child was passing through their pristine waters on a stolen boat.

A couple on a lit deck raised wine glasses in their direction. Assuming they were neighbors out for an evening cruise.

Anne didn't wave back.

"Contacts, starboard!" one of Hull's men called out.

Motorcycle headlights weaving along the shoreline road, beams cutting the dark. Coordinated. Persistent. Paralleling their course.

"How many?" Hull checked his weapon despite his condition.

"Four visible. Probably more in the trees." She pushed the throttle. "They're good. Spread out, using terrain."

"Can you lose them?"

"Not on open water. But there's a beach access north. Shallow water, rocks. They'll have to dismount."

Hull swayed. "Do it. I've probably got thirty minutes of fight left before this becomes academic."

"You'll be fine. Folks like us don't die."

"Not worried about me." His eyes went toward the cabin. The girl.

Anne's jaw tightened. She didn't say what she was thinking.

The beach access opened ahead. A narrow channel between rocks. Anne throttled back, reading the water for obstacles the way she read streets for trouble. Hull's men lifted the girl from the cabin and moved through the surf. Anne vaulted over the side into knee-deep water. The cold hit her like a fist.

"Which way?" she asked Hull as he stumbled onto sand.

"North. Extraction point two clicks through the trees."

They crashed through underbrush in the dark. Moonlight through the canopy. Mansion lights through the trees. Behind them, voices calling coordinates. The pursuers had night vision and radio coordination, and Anne had a courier bag and the ability to run faster than a bleeding soldier.

Muzzle flashes lit the dark behind them. Automatic weapons fire cutting through the air close enough that she could feel the pressure of it against her eardrums.

Hull dropped to one knee, returning fire. "Keep moving! Get the package to the road!"

The service road appeared ahead. Narrow asphalt. Vehicles waiting, engines running.

Then the gunfire stopped.

Not tapered off. Stopped. The voices behind them went silent. The motorcycle engines faded. The night changed from combat to quiet in the space of a heartbeat, as if someone had turned a dial and shut the whole thing off.

Hull straightened despite his wounds. His weapon lowered. "We're clear."

They broke from the treeline.

Two black vehicles. Positioned with the precision of someone who planned arrivals the way architects planned load-bearing walls. Drivers, security, everything clean and competent and radiating a level of operational control that made Hull's convoy look like a school trip.

A woman stood beside the lead vehicle.

Anne's first thought was that she was small. Not short, exactly. Compact. But the space around her was wrong. People who were standing ten feet away from her were leaning away from her, the way grass leans from a fire that hasn't reached it yet. The drivers had oriented their vehicles around her position. The security team had arranged itself in a geometry that put her at the center without putting her in the center. She wasn't standing in a protected position. She was standing in the position everything else was organized to protect.

Blonde hair pulled back in a tight knot. Steel gray eyes. No insignia. No rank. A rifle in her hands, held the way a carpenter holds a hammer. Not threatening. Just present. The tool of someone who used it so often it had become part of her silhouette.

The motorcycles behind them roared. Not closer. Away. One by one, turning around. Leaving. Armed pursuit teams with automatic weapons and night vision, pulling back like water receding from a coast.

Because of her.

Hull snapped to attention despite his injuries. The automatic response of a career soldier in the presence of something that outranked rank.

"Ma'am," he said.

"Commander." Quiet. The kind of voice that didn't need volume because it had never been ignored. "Status report."

"Cargo secured. Minimal complications during extraction." He gestured toward the girl. "Courier performed above expectations."

"Minimal? Half your team's down, and you're leaking like a sieve."

"Slightly minimal complications, Ma'am."

"Go find a spot to sit until I can get a good look at you. Try not to ruin anything with your blood."

The woman's gaze found Anne.

It was like being walked through. Not examined. Not assessed. Walked through, room by room, by someone who could read the layout of a building just by looking at the front door. Anne felt her spine straighten and didn't decide to do it. Her body responding to whatever signal this woman broadcast, the way a compass needle responds to north.

"Ms. Calder." Not a question. "Your reputation precedes you."

Anne's hands were at her sides. She made herself keep them there. Every instinct she had was telling her two things at once: this woman was the most dangerous person she had ever been in a room with, and this woman already knew everything about her that mattered.

The woman gestured toward the vehicles. "Shall we proceed? There's much to discuss."

Hull's men loaded the girl into the second vehicle. Anne watched. The dark braids. The small body. The sedated stillness of a child being transferred between adults who had decided her future without asking her opinion.

Anne got in the vehicle. The door closed.

The Marks faded in the rearview mirror. Hull leaned against the passenger door, finally letting the strain show. The road ahead was dark.

In the vehicle behind them, a girl with amber eyes rode toward whatever "evaluation and processing" meant in this woman's world.

Anne watched the road and said nothing.

I, MARKED

PART THREE

NEW VARIABLES

Late Autumn, 2173

Safe House, Northern Territory, outside Reed's Harbor, CA

The safe house was a two-story clapboard at the end of a gravel drive that hadn't seen maintenance in years. Anne clocked it on approach: one door visible from the front, ground-floor windows on three sides, second-floor windows smaller and set higher. The kind of building that looked abandoned until you noticed the new deadbolt on the front door and the fresh tire tracks in the mud.

Inside: dust, mildew, stale coffee. Government furniture. The kind of place that existed in bureaucratic blind spots for conversations that couldn't happen in official buildings.

Anne counted the rooms as they moved through. Front room. Kitchen through a narrow doorway, back door visible but chained from the inside. Hallway leading to a staircase. She noted the lock on the back door. Padlock, not deadbolt. The windows in the front room were painted shut. She could tell by the blistered seam where the frame met the sash. The glass was old, single-pane. Breakable, if it came to that.

The walls were plaster over lath. She could hear Hull's boots on the floor above her. Which meant she could hear everything in this house, and everything in this house could hear her.

She took a chair by the window. Not the most comfortable seat. The one with the best view of the door and the driveway and the tree line beyond it.

Rain streaked down the glass. Pre-dawn gray.

"What did you get yourself into this time?" Shori asked behind her.

Anne caught it in the window's reflection: Shori cleaning the shrapnel wounds on Hull's arm, movements careful, precise. Not medical training. Something closer to habit. The kind of care that came from having done this for the same person more times than either of them wanted to count.

"Just a scratch," Hull growled.

"Scratches don't need sutures." Shori threaded a needle. "Your stubbornness will get you killed."

"Won't have to endure any more of these conversations then."

Shori pulled the suture tight. Hull didn't flinch. Anne watched their reflections move around each other with the particular ease of people who'd shared space for a long time. Not romantic, necessarily. But deep. The kind of relationship where you stopped explaining yourself years ago because the other person already knew.

"You should have called for backup the moment the operation was compromised," Shori said. "This was supposed to be a simple relocation."

"Simple relocations don't require three-vehicle escorts and tactical teams." Hull winked at Anne in the window's reflection. "We got caught advertising. Someone knew we were coming."

Shori's hands stilled. Just for a moment. Then resumed. "Explain."

"Ambush was too well coordinated. They knew the route, the timing, probably the cargo. Military precision. Not random criminals."

"Any idea who?"

"Freehold remnants have the gear and the grudges. Corporate labs keep sniffing around anything connected to the girl. Hell, even family loyalists might try something stupid." Hull winced as she secured the bandage. "Lots of people want what we're moving. Not a lot of them are polite about it."

"The girl's family is out of that equation," Shori said quietly.

Hull's expression didn't change. His shoulders did. Acceptance, not surprise.

"What about the route?" Shori reached for bandaging material. "Who had access?"

"Standard distribution. Command staff, vehicle commanders, the courier." His eyes flicked toward Anne. "New variable in the equation."

Anne kept her gaze on the window. She could feel the weight of their attention the way you feel a change in air pressure. They weren't accusing her. Not yet. They were positioning her, the way you position a piece on a board before you decide what it's worth.

The conversation shifted to logistics. Communications analysis. External threats. Institutional language that treated the night's violence as a problem with a solution somewhere in the paperwork. Anne let it wash over her and counted the seconds between the rain hitting the glass and the drops reaching the sill. Seventeen. The window leaked.

Hull's voice was starting to slur. Painkillers. Shori noticed before Anne did.

"There's a room upstairs," Shori said. "Clean beds, secure perimeter. Try not to break my needlework, and don't bleed on the white linen. You know that never fully comes out."

Hull pushed himself up. "What about the courier?"

"Ms. Calder can rest as well. We'll have more to discuss once everyone's had time to process."

Anne turned from the window as Hull made his way toward the staircase. He moved like someone who'd been through this loop before: injured, patched, sent to recover while the adults figured out what the damage meant.

Shori watched him go. Then she checked the locks, adjusted the blinds, moved through the space with the automatic efficiency of someone whose security sweep was muscle memory.

"Long night," she said, settling into Hull's chair.

"Longer than most."

"But profitable, I hope?"

Anne met her gaze for the first time since the safe house. "About that. The payment we discussed. I completed the job, got your cargo delivered despite complications. I'd like to settle up and head back to Beltmoire."

The courtesy didn't leave Shori's face. It cooled. Like frost forming on the inside of a window.

"Of course," Shori said. She reached into her jacket and withdrew an envelope. "You performed admirably under difficult circumstances."

She extended it. Anne reached for it. Relief flooding through her at the idea of finishing this and going home.

Shori didn't let go.

"However." Still polite. Still professional. The steel underneath it showing through like rebar through cracked concrete. "I'm afraid you're not going anywhere just yet."

Anne's hand stilled on the envelope.

"There are questions about tonight's events. Security concerns. Someone compromised the operation. Someone knew details they shouldn't have." Shori's tone stayed conversational. "Until we determine who and how, everyone involved remains available."

"I was hired for courier work. I couried. The work is complete."

"You were also the newest variable in a carefully planned operation that went sideways in ways that suggest inside information." Shori released the envelope. Anne took it. "That makes you either a very unfortunate coincidence or a very useful lead."

"Either way, Lieutenant Voss will be here shortly." Shori settled back. "I'm told he has extensive experience in these matters."

Anne flinched. She couldn't stop it. Voss. The name carried a specific kind of weight in Beltmoire. Mob enforcer. The kind who specialized in work other criminals wouldn't touch.

Shori noticed. "I see his reputation precedes him."

"I know the name."

"Good. That should make things efficient."

The rain had stopped. The gray morning that replaced it looked about as permanent as Anne's options.

✧

She woke to voices downstairs and the uncomfortable fact that someone had been watching her sleep.

Rika sat in a chair by the door. Rifle across her lap. Studying Anne with the focused attention of someone who'd been doing this for hours.

The same Rika who'd been crouched in the back seat last night, returning fire while Anne drove them through a kill zone.

"Morning," Rika said. Flat. Her eyes flicked to the floor. "You can use the bathroom, but the door stays open. Breakfast is downstairs when you're ready."

Anne sat up. Noted the way Rika's jaw tightened when their eyes met. The space between them charged with something neither of them was going to name.

"Aren't I lucky to have saved your ass back there?"

Rika's grip shifted on the rifle.

"Orders are orders," she said. "Nothing personal."

"Right." Anne swung her legs off the bed. "Feels personal, though, doesn't it."

She moved through her morning routine under observation. Bathroom with the door open. Rika maintaining distance that was respectful and unmistakable and made escape impossible. Anne washed her face and studied the bathroom while the water ran. Small window above the toilet. Frosted glass. She could fit through it. Barely. Eight-foot drop to a mud patch on the north side of the building, based on the sound of the rain earlier. She filed it away.

The voices downstairs had grown louder by the time she descended. Shori's measured tones mixing with something harsher. Something that grated.

Anne paused on the stairs. The fourth step from the bottom creaked. She noted it. Then she noted the front room from above: the chair layout had changed. More seats, arranged in a loose semicircle facing the center of the room. A woman stood in the far corner who hadn't been there last night. Auburn hair tied back. Green eyes moving across the room with quiet precision. Cataloging. Filing.

Rika gestured her toward the main room.

The dynamic had changed completely.

Shori stood by the window where Anne had been sitting, but her attention was focused on a man who filled the room the way a bad smell fills a room. Not with size. With presence that made you wish for fresh air.

Short. Stocky. A horseshoe fringe of graying hair around a scalp pocked with old acne scars. His left leg carried a limp he tried to hide by never standing still. Fingers tapping his thigh in rapid patterns. Nervous rhythms that didn't match the authority in his voice.

Anne's body read him before her brain finished the profile. The tremor in his hands wasn't nerves. It was need. Chemical. The constant movement, the tapping, the way his energy ran ahead of his words. She'd seen it on the streets. People who functioned on something that kept them sharp and ate them from the inside.

"Not saying she planned it from the beginning," he was saying. His voice had the theatrical weight of a man who'd practiced being intimidating until it became a personality. "But opportunities present themselves, and clever dumb people capitalize on opportunities."

His eyes found Anne. His lips pulled back. It might have been a smile if it had contained any warmth.

"Speaking of clever people. Ms. Calder, I presume?"

Anne nodded.

"Marty Voss." He extended a hand. The tremor was almost invisible unless you were looking for it. His grip lingered a beat too long. When she pulled back, his eyes stayed on her, then flicked away.

"Young woman, new to the game, shows up just when things go sideways." Sharper now. "Convenient, don't you think?"

Anne stayed standing. Every chair in the room would put her lower than Voss. He'd arranged it that way, or the room had been arranged for him by someone who understood what he needed.

"This is Nessa Kaine," Shori said, gesturing toward the woman in the corner. "Intelligence specialist. She'll be assisting with the investigation."

Nessa was tall. Composed. Dark auburn hair, practical ponytail, clothes that managed to look professional and forgettable at the same time. Where Voss grabbed attention, Nessa absorbed it. Her green eyes didn't demand. They processed.

She nodded at Anne but didn't offer her hand.

"Ms. Calder." Neutral. Courteous. Giving nothing. "I understand last night was your first job with this particular client base."

"That's right."

"Interesting timing," Voss cut in. His leg bounced. "First job, biggest security breach they've had in years. Makes a person wonder about cause and effect."

"You're suggesting I set up the ambush?" Anne asked.

"I'm suggesting," Voss said, leaning forward, "that opportunity knocked and you answered. Think about it. Courier work doesn't clear serious debts. But information about high-value cargo moving through predictable routes? That's worth real money to the right people."

He was smart. Crude and unpleasant, but smart. Anne could see how the narrative fit together from the outside: new courier, desperate finances, convenient timing, inside access.

"Who would I sell information to?" she asked.

"Freehold types have deep pockets and long memories," Nessa said. First time she'd spoken since introductions. "Corporate labs pay well for anything that gets them an edge. And family networks with the right motivation can pull together more money than you'd think." She shrugged. "Plenty of buyers. Not a lot of them are picky about their sources."

The words were casual. The phrasing was street. But Anne caught something underneath it. Nessa's list was too clean. Too organized. Like someone who'd rehearsed casual and landed just north of it.

"The beauty of it," Voss continued, warming to his theory, "is that you don't even have to pick sides. Sell the route information, collect payment, show up for the job anyway. If the buyers succeed, you get paid twice. If they fail, you still get courier fees and nobody looks at the girl who was just doing her job."

He stood. His limp was worse when he'd been sitting. He paced around the room and Anne tracked his movement while watching Shori and Nessa hold position. Three points of a triangle with Anne at the center.

"The operation began in UAD Beltmoire..."

"That's Beltmoire, Union bitch," Anne and Voss said at the same time.

The correction landed in the room like a slap. Voss's eyes snapped to Anne. Hers to his. A beat of recognition between two people who shared a vocabulary they hadn't expected to share.

Shori continued as if nothing had happened. "With a carefully planned route that somehow became known to hostile forces. The problem is that the buyers didn't fail completely. They got the information they wanted, but they didn't get the cargo. So now we have a situation where someone made money selling intelligence, and we still have our asset secured."

"Perfect crime, really." Voss's eyes were sharp. Whatever was running through his system kept his mind cutting even when his body twitched. "If you hadn't been so obviously new, nobody would have looked at you twice."

"What evidence do you have?" Anne asked.

His laugh was short. "Evidence? Sweetheart, you're the evidence. New face, financial problems, perfect timing, and now you're in a safe house instead of heading back to whatever hole you crawled out of in Beltmoire."

"That's because you won't let me leave."

"Because smart people don't let potential security breaches walk," Shori said. "The question isn't whether you can leave. The question is what you did to compromise last night's operation."

Anne looked at the three of them. The investigator with the tremor. The operative by the window. The intelligence specialist in the corner who was playing a role Anne hadn't fully identified yet. Three people who'd already decided what had happened and were now building the box around the conclusion.

"So what happens now?" Anne asked.

"Now," Voss said, settling back into his chair, "we investigate. Trace communications. Check financial records. Talk to people." His smile widened. "And we see what kind of story comes together when we shake the pieces."

He pushed himself up, stretching his bad leg. "Well, this has been educational, but I've got things to do, and I need to piss." He moved toward the door, pausing to look back. "You ladies have fun while I'm gone. Let's stick to the facts when I get back."

His laugh echoed down the hallway.

The room changed the moment he left. Like pressure dropping before a storm. Voss's crude theater had been filling the space, and without it, the silence that replaced it had edges.

Anne was facing two women who had their own conversation planned for this moment. And whatever came next was going to be considerably more sophisticated than Voss's blunt theater.

PART FOUR

THE BREAKING POINT

Late Autumn, 2173

Safe House, Northern Territory

— ❖ —

The room changed the moment Voss left it. Quieter, but not safer. Like the difference between a noisy bar and an empty alley.

Shori moved to the window. Back to the room. Nessa shifted closer to Anne. Casual. The kind of movement that wanted to look accidental.

"He's a pig," Nessa said quietly. "The way he talks to women. Disgusting."

Anne stayed standing. Every chair in the room was lower than the two women. She wasn't sitting. "He's honest about what he is."

"Fair point." Nessa's smile was warm. Almost conspiratorial. "Look, Anne, can I call you Anne? I think we got off on the wrong foot here. I'm not like them." She gestured toward Shori's back. "I didn't grow up in some Union academy looking down at the rest of the world."

"No?"

"Hell no. I came up the hard way. Same as you. Started running numbers outside Hammison when I was twelve, worked my way up to petty crime, then breaking and entering. Eventually found my way to off-market intel through brokering." Nessa leaned against the wall. Settling in. "I know what it's like to have people in suits assume you're stupid because you talk different."

Anne watched her. The accent had shifted. Rougher edges showing up that hadn't been there during the formal interrogation. Could be real. Could be another layer.

"The thing is," Nessa continued, "Voss is setting you up to take the fall for something bigger than a route compromise. He needs a scapegoat, and you're convenient." She dropped her voice. "But that doesn't mean you have to play along."

Nessa's eyes flicked to Shori. Just for a beat. The kind of check-in that people do when they're running a play and want to make sure the other person is still on script.

Shori turned from the window. "Ms. Kaine, perhaps you should—"

"What? Tell her pretty lies about how this is all going to work out fine?" Nessa's voice carried enough edge to sound like defiance. "She's not stupid. She knows this investigation is bullshit."

Anne watched the interplay. Nessa positioning herself as the reasonable one. The ally against the cold authority and the crude enforcer. The person who understood Anne because she'd come from the same streets.

Good cop wasn't a strong enough word. This was a performance. And Nessa was good at it.

"You're both cut from the same cloth," Anne said. "Just different tailoring."

Nessa laughed. It didn't quite land. "Come on. Look at her." She nodded toward Shori. "Union operative in an expensive coat. Never had to wonder where her next meal was coming from. You think she understands what it's like to survive under the boot of the Union?"

"Careful, Ms. Kaine," Shori said.

"Why? Because I'm telling the truth?" Nessa turned back to Anne. "She's got no authority here except what the mob gives her. This whole operation is a joint venture. Union needs mob cooperation to move through territories they don't control."

Anne filed it. Not because she believed it. Because the information Nessa was choosing to share told her more than the information itself.

"Here's what I think happened," Nessa said. "Someone in the Union hierarchy leaked the route. Someone with access to planning documents, schedules, cargo manifests. But they can't investigate their own people without admitting their security is compromised. So they need an outsider to pin it on."

The theory was better than Voss's. That made it more dangerous, not less.

"Why tell me this?" Anne asked.

"Because the mob doesn't appreciate being used as cleanup crew for Union mistakes." Something that sounded like genuine anger. "And because maybe you saw something that could help us figure out which Union bastard really set this up."

The hook.

Anne recognized it because her mother had taught her to recognize it. The offer that felt like help but was shaped like a funnel: wide at the top where they let you talk, narrow at the bottom where they use what you gave them.

"I told you what happened," Anne said. "I drove the route, we got ambushed, I helped get everyone out alive."

"But you're smart," Nessa pressed. "You had to notice things. Inconsistencies." She leaned forward. "Things that might help us figure out who really set this up."

Shori had moved from the window. Circling behind Anne's position. Pressure from two directions now. The reasonable ally in front. The cold authority behind. Forcing Anne to split her attention.

"Did you notice anything unusual about the attackers?" Nessa asked. "Equipment, tactics, coordination?"

"Professional setup," Anne said. "Military precision and gear."

"Exactly. Not random criminals. Someone with serious resources and inside knowledge." Nessa's voice carried satisfaction. "Someone who knew exactly when and where to strike."

"Someone like you," Anne said.

Quiet. Low. But it landed like a brick through a window.

Nessa's posture changed. Not dramatically. A stiffening through the shoulders, a micro-adjustment in her weight distribution. The mob-intelligence stance losing a fraction of its slouch.

"What's that supposed to mean?" Nessa asked. But something in the vowels had shifted. The rough edges smoothing out, just slightly.

And Anne felt it happen. The thing she'd been sitting on for the last twenty minutes, all the details that didn't fit, all the micro-observations she'd been cataloguing without deciding to, all the reads that had been stacking up since she'd walked into this room. It broke loose.

Not organized. Not a speech. It came out the way water comes out of a cracked pipe: fast, pressurized, and pointed at whoever was standing closest.

"Your accent's wrong." She turned on Nessa first. "You had it for the first five minutes, then you lost it when you started talking about Freehold types. Real runners from Beltmoire don't say 'financial resources.' They say 'Freeholers got cash.' And you keep checking her before you talk." She jabbed a finger toward Shori. "Every time. Like you're looking for permission, or confirmation, or something. Colleagues don't do that. Partners do."

Nessa opened her mouth.

Anne wasn't done.

"And you." She turned to Shori. "You fuss over Hull's wounds like he's yours. You know where the medical supplies are without looking. You know this house. You've been here before. Probably a lot. But your story is that the mob runs this territory and you're Union, so what are you doing in a mob safe house that you know better than your own coat pockets?"

Her breath was coming faster. She could feel herself losing the thread, the observations tumbling out faster than she could organize them. But she couldn't stop it. Three years of reading people, of surviving by seeing what other people missed, and it was all spilling at once.

"You move the same way she does." Anne's voice was shaking. Not fear. Adrenaline. The sheer physical intensity of saying things out loud that she should have been smart enough to keep to herself. "Same corners. Same angles. The way you orient in a room. The way you track each other's positions without looking. That's not mob and Union playing nice. That's two people who know each other's bodies."

The word hung in the air.

"You're not business partners," Anne said. "You're together."

You see people as they truly are when they think you're beneath them.

Her mother's voice. Quiet. Under everything. The second time, and it arrived not as a lesson but as confirmation. This was what the training was for. This room. This moment. Seeing through the performance to the architecture underneath it.

"And this whole thing," Anne continued, "the investigation, the scapegoat, Voss's little show, all of it. It's not about finding who leaked the route. It's about making sure nobody looks too hard at the people who planned it."

Silence.

Then Hull's voice from the doorway.

"Preach it, sister."

He was leaning against the frame with a toasted bagel in his good hand. Peanut butter and processed cheese. He took a bite, chewing with the placid contentment of a man who'd been listening from the kitchen and was enjoying every second of what he'd heard.

Anne looked at him. Looked at Shori, whose hands had gone white-knuckled on the chair back. Looked at Nessa, whose carefully constructed persona was hanging off her like a coat that didn't fit anymore.

"The only genuine person in this room is this guy," Anne said, pointing at Hull. "And he has the audacity to put peanut butter and processed cheese on a bagel."

Hull dusted crumbs off his sling. "Don't be a hater."

"Lady," Anne said to Shori, "staring down hijackers with nothing but your bitchface and a rifle is impressive. But you suck. You and your Union can go piss on an electric fence for all I care."

She turned to Nessa. Her voice changed. Not softer. Different. Something that might have been respect, buried under the anger. "And as for you, Ms. Kaine. I got no quarrel with you. Takes real guts to play both sides the way you're doing. That's a dangerous game."

She stepped back. "Keep your secrets. Just make sure there's enough left standing for the rest of us when the dust settles."

The room held its breath.

Shori's hand was on the chair back. Her knuckles hadn't loosened.

PART FIVE

THE REVELATION

Late Autumn, 2173

Safe House, Northern Territory

Hull settled into a chair with the air of a man who'd found better entertainment than sleep. Shori hadn't moved. Nessa was standing very still, her mob posture abandoned somewhere in the last sixty seconds, her actual posture showing through: straight-backed, precise, the stance of someone with training she hadn't acquired on any street.

Then Shori moved.

Not the way she'd been moving. Not careful. Not measured. Fast. Fluid. The kind of motion that had made armed pursuit teams disappear into the dark. She crossed the room in three steps, kicked the rifle from its position against the wall into her hands, and leveled it at Anne's face.

Anne's breath stopped. The barrel was close enough that she could see the rifling inside it.

"You think you're clever." Shori's voice was different. Stripped. The courtesy gone, the professional coolness gone, just the raw thing underneath, and the raw thing was terrifying. "You think you've figured something out."

The woman who'd fussed over Hull's stitches was gone. This was the person who'd stood on a dark road and made armed men choose to leave. The person who'd said the girl's family was "out of the equation" with a voice that explained exactly what that meant.

Her finger rested outside the trigger guard. Discipline. But Anne could see the tension in the tendon. Wanting.

"The problem with clever girls," Shori said, stepping closer, "is that they don't understand the difference between being smart and being useful. And right now, you're proving to be significantly more trouble than—"

"Yo, take that shit outside." Hull didn't look up. He was examining his bagel. "You just yelled at me about getting blood on the linen. You thought about how hard it is getting brain matter out of the cushions?"

Nessa's hand found Shori's arm. Not grabbing. Asking.

"Enough," she said. Quiet.

Shori stopped.

And that told Anne more than anything else in the last twenty-four hours. Nessa's hand on Shori's arm. One word. And the most dangerous person Anne had ever been in a room with lowered a rifle she'd been ready to use.

Shori stepped back. The rifle stayed in her hands but the barrel dropped. Her eyes didn't leave Anne's face.

"This complicates everything," she said. "We needed someone who would take the blame quietly. Not someone who can see through operational security."

"Maybe that's not entirely a bad thing," Nessa said.

When she spoke, her voice was different. The mob drawl was gone. Not fading, not slipping. Gone. What replaced it was crisp. Direct. A voice that carried authority the way a good foundation carries a building: without effort, without performance, without needing anyone to notice it was there.

"Sit down, Anne," Nessa said.

"I'm good where I am."

"You made several accurate observations." Nessa was studying her. Not the calculating assessment from before. Something closer to curiosity. "How long have you been reading people like this?"

"Long enough to stay alive."

"We're trained to make people see what we want them to see. You figured us out in twenty minutes." Nessa shook her head. "Most people never see past the surface."

"Survival skill," Anne said. "People lie with their mouths, but their bodies tell the truth."

"Like Voss's trembling fingers."

Anne's eyes sharpened. "You noticed that too."

A beat of recognition between them. Two people who'd learned to survive by seeing through the same lies. But Anne wasn't ready to trust recognition. Recognition was just another tool people used to get you to lower your guard.

Shori set the rifle against the wall. Her expression had hardened into something calculating. "What we need is to close this investigation and move on. We can't have someone walking around with this level of awareness. Someone crude. With grievances."

The word "crude" landed deliberately. Anne heard what was underneath it. Not an insult. A category. Expendable people. People who could be removed without institutional cost.

"Your convoy still got compromised," Anne said. "Someone with inside access sold you out. You're just mad because I proved it wasn't me."

"You proved you're observant," Shori corrected. "That doesn't prove innocence."

"It proves I'm not the easy mark you thought I was."

Hull had stopped eating. His earlier entertainment was fading into something more watchful. "You ladies figure this out soon? Putting me to sleep."

"The real question," Shori said, "is what we do now."

Anne felt the room tilt toward something permanent. The conversation had moved past interrogation, past scapegoating, past the investigation entirely. Shori was calculating whether Anne was a problem that could be contained or a problem that needed to be eliminated.

"You could just let me go," Anne said. "I did the job. Got your cargo delivered. We call it even."

"Unfortunately, it's not that simple anymore."

No one spoke. The safe house settled around them. The creak of old wood. The sound of Hull shifting in his chair.

Heavy footsteps in the hallway. More than one pair.

Voss returning. And he wasn't alone.

PART SIX

THE EVIDENCE

Late Autumn, 2173

Safe House, Northern Territory

The heavy footsteps grew louder. Voss's uneven gait and at least two other sets of boots. The door opened and he entered with the energy of a man who'd brought ammunition.

"Ladies." His eyes swept the room. Whatever tension he was reading, he chose to interpret it as progress. "I hope you've had a productive conversation."

Nessa stepped back from Anne. The crisp posture dissolved. The mob slouch returned. The nervous energy of someone navigating between competing authorities settled over her like a coat she'd taken off and was now shrugging back on. She didn't look at Anne. But her hand adjusted at her side, a single finger tapping once against her thigh. A beat. An acknowledgment.

Shori moved from the wall. The rifle was still in her hands but held differently now. Equipment. The government operative managing an investigation, not the woman who'd been ready to paint the cushions.

"Lieutenant," Shori said. Neutral. "Were you able to verify the financial records?"

"More than verify." Voss reached into his jacket and withdrew a folder. Substantial. He held it the way a man holds something he's proud of. "Turns out our little courier has been busier than she let on. Banking records show three deposits in the past month that don't match any documented courier jobs."

Anne's stomach dropped. She had no idea what he'd manufactured, but she could see the shape of it. Unexplained income. Timing that aligned with the operation. A story that fit together from the outside even if none of it was true.

"Interesting," Nessa said. Mob drawl. Perfect. "What kind of amounts?"

"Enough to clear debt with Beltmoire bookmakers." Voss was smiling. "The kind of payments that show up when someone talks too much to Freehold types or corporate labs."

Hull yawned. Stretched. Reached into his cargo pocket with the unhurried movement of someone looking for a stick of gum.

"The timeline fits perfectly," Voss continued. "First deposit three weeks ago, second two weeks ago, third five days before our operation. Someone was paying for advance intelligence on our transport route."

"That's bullshit," Anne said.

"Is it?" Voss spread documents across the table. Flourish. Presentation. "Bank records don't lie, sweetheart. Numbers tell a story, and yours is looking pretty rich."

"Hells, you bore me," Hull said.

He pulled a crumpled report from his pocket. Wrinkled. Folded wrong. The kind of paper that had been sitting against his hip since before Voss left the building.

Voss stopped. His eyes went to the paper.

"Intelligence report," Hull said, reading from it with the flat tone of someone reciting a grocery list. "Culprit was a guard in the lead car. Blown up with his own intel. They killed their own informant."

Silence.

Anne watched Voss's face. Surprise. Calculation. Something that wanted to be disappointment but settled for acceptance. Fast. The man adapted like breathing.

"Well." He forced a smile. "That's convenient. Inside information from security personnel rather than civilian contractors. That would explain the precision of the ambush."

"Dead informant can't contradict anything," Voss added, already pivoting. "Convenient for everyone involved."

"Dead like this conversation," Hull said.

"Very convenient," Shori agreed. Something in her tone suggested she didn't believe convenience had anything to do with it. "In light of this, Ms. Calder, you're free to go. The investigation will focus on the compromised guard."

"Bloody Union thugs," Nessa said. Right amount of disgust. Right amount of contempt. "No morals. Turn their own people into informants, then kill them when it's useful."

Anne heard it. The performance was flawless. Nessa had taken the lesson from twenty minutes ago, the one about how real street runners talked, and fed it back through her mob character without a seam showing. She was learning from Anne in real time. That should have been flattering. Instead it made the hair on Anne's arms stand up.

"Indeed," Voss said. He gathered his useless evidence. The frustration was visible in the way he aligned the papers, too precisely, the gesture of someone imposing order on a situation that had slipped out of his control. "I suppose that concludes our business. Ms. Calder, I trust you'll be more careful about your client selection."

"I'll keep that in mind."

He moved toward the door. Paused. Looked back. His eyes stayed on Anne a beat too long, and what she saw in them wasn't acceptance. It was postponement.

"Ladies. Gentlemen. Always a pleasure."

"I'll walk you out," Shori said.

Their voices faded down the hallway. The outer door opened and closed. Anne was alone with Hull and Nessa.

Nobody spoke.

When Shori returned, the rifle was still in her hands. Her attention found Anne and stayed there.

"I should go," Anne said.

"Yes." Shori's agreement didn't sound like permission. "You should."

She stepped closer. Not the explosive lunge from before. Controlled. Deliberate. The woman who planned things.

"Remember, little one." Low. Sharp. "You're alive for a reason. Don't test it."

Nessa moved forward. "We'll be in touch," she said.

Four words. Simple. But they carried the weight of a door opening onto something Anne couldn't see the shape of yet.

Anne looked at Hull. "You're an ass, you know that? I nearly got my brains blown out while you were picking at your bandages."

"But you didn't." Cheerful. "And now you're free to go. You're welcome."

She gathered her courier bag and walked down the hall. As she reached the door, Hull's voice followed her.

"Interesting morning. Can you believe she is only twelve?"

Anne stepped outside. Gray afternoon. The rain had stopped but the air was still wet, heavy, the kind of cold that got into your jacket and stayed.

Voss's sedan was idling at the end of the drive. Exhaust rising in the cold air. Two figures in the back seat.

Voss rolled down the passenger window. His smile was visible from fifty feet away.

"Kid," he called out. "Get in."

I, MARKED

PART SEVEN

MARKED

Late Autumn, 2173

Open Highway – Southbound towards Beltmoire

The ride started in silence.

Anne sat in the passenger seat of Voss's sedan and watched the countryside roll past through rain-streaked windows. Two of his men occupied the back seat. They hadn't spoken since she'd gotten in, but the way they sat, the way their weight was distributed, the way their hands rested where hands rest when they're ready to move fast. This wasn't a ride home.

She tried the door handle. Casual. Like she was adjusting her position.

It didn't move.

Child locks. She didn't know when he'd activated them. Maybe before she'd gotten in. Maybe they'd never been off.

Voss drove with his fingers tapping the wheel. The same nervous rhythm she'd been reading since the safe house, but the energy underneath it was different. Not the chemical jitter. Something colder. The controlled tension of a man who'd been making a decision for the last thirty miles and had just finished making it.

The landscape was changing. Fewer houses. Longer stretches between crossroads. Forest pressing close on both sides of the road. The kind of emptiness that existed for people who needed it.

"Hell of a thing," Voss said finally. "Investigation getting wrapped up so neat and tidy."

Anne kept her eyes on the window. Fifty miles from Beltmoire, according to the last sign. "Lucky break."

"Lucky." No humor in the laugh. "Amazing how these intelligence reports just appear when they're needed most."

She said nothing. Her heart was doing something it hadn't done during the ambush or the interrogation or the moment Shori leveled a rifle at her face. It was beating faster, but quietly. The adrenaline wasn't spiking. It was pooling. Gathering in her stomach like cold water filling a basin.

"Something bothering you about it?" she asked. Testing.

"You saw something in that room." Sharp. The pretense dropping the way a coat drops when you stop pretending you're cold. "You know that Nessa Kaine's too perfect. Too new. What do you know about her?"

In the rearview mirror, one of the men in the back seat checked his watch. Not boredom. Coordination. They were on a schedule.

"I know you're fishing," Anne said. "Just like your fabricated evidence."

"Was it fabricated?" He glanced at her. No pretense left at all. "How would you know? You never saw the documents."

The casual admission. He wasn't hiding that the evidence was manufactured. He was telling her he knew she knew, and he was watching to see what she did with that.

"The investigation is closed," Anne said.

"The official investigation." He corrected her the way he corrected everything: with precision and the implication that precision was a weapon. "My personal investigation is just getting started."

Another mile marker. Forty-five miles from safety. She tested the window controls. Dead.

"What really happened in that room after I left?" Voss's voice had settled into something focused. Methodical. The voice of a man who extracted things from people for a living. "Because when I walked out, you were a liability about to be eliminated. When I walked back in, suddenly you're walking free and everyone's acting like you might have value. That kind of turnaround doesn't happen by accident."

"I think everyone involved has secrets."

"Very diplomatic." His smile cut. "I'm not interested in diplomacy."

The sedan slowed.

Anne saw the sign: REST AREA — 1 MILE.

Her stomach dropped. She pressed her palms against her thighs to stop the shaking.

"Where are we going?"

"Somewhere we can have a proper conversation."

The rest area appeared ahead. Isolated highway stop. Picnic tables, restrooms, a gravel lot screened from the highway by trees. Empty. No other vehicles. No witnesses.

Voss pulled into the farthest corner and killed the engine.

"You know what really bothers me?" he said, turning to face her. "It's not the investigation. Investigations are just paperwork. What bothers me is that I had a very specific plan for how last night was supposed to go. A contingency. Months of work. The right people in the right positions, waiting for the right moment."

He reached into his jacket and withdrew something. Not a gun. Small. Metal. A cylinder with surgical markings etched into its surface. He held it the way you'd hold a tool you'd used many times.

"And then some twelve-year-old courier from Beltmoire decided to improvise."

The words landed. Anne felt them hit, felt the shape of what he was saying before the meaning fully assembled.

The ambush. The route compromise. Voss hadn't been investigating the leak.

Voss WAS the leak.

He'd arranged for the girl to be intercepted. His people. His plan. The attackers with military precision and no insignia. And when the ambush went wrong, when Anne threw the convoy off-route and through The Marks and onto a stolen boat and delivered the cargo to Shori's extraction point instead of wherever Voss needed it to go, she hadn't just saved the girl.

She'd cost him everything.

"That girl was worth more than you'll make in ten lifetimes," Voss said. His voice was flat. The theatrical personality stripped away. Just the man underneath. "I had buyers. Serious people with serious resources. The kind of people who don't accept failure as an answer."

The thermecine injector turned slowly in his fingers.

"And now I have to explain to those serious people why their investment went sideways because a child who can barely see over the steering wheel decided to play hero."

"I was doing my job," Anne said. Her voice came out steadier than she felt. "Your job too, if you hadn't been selling out your own convoy."

Something changed in his face. Not anger. Past anger. The flat expression of a man who'd moved through fury into the kind of cold that makes decisions.

"Someone protected you in that room," he said. "Someone decided you were worth keeping. I want to know who."

"I don't know what you're talking about."

"The beauty of this," Voss said, holding up the injector, "isn't just what it does to your eye. It's what it does to your credibility. Who's going to believe a broken, disfigured courier when she starts making accusations about respected operatives?"

"Last chance." Finality. "Tell me who protected you and why, and maybe I'll make this quick."

Anne looked at the thermecine injector. Looked at Voss. Looked at the empty rest area and the trees and the highway that was too far away and the two men in the back seat who were already moving.

"Go to hell."

"Wrong answer," Voss said quietly.

✧

The doors opened at the same time.

Hands grabbed her from both sides. Anne fought. She kicked at the man on her left and connected with his knee. He grunted and his grip loosened and she twisted free for half a second, long enough to get one foot on the gravel and throw an elbow at the man on her right.

It connected. Cartilage crunched. Someone swore.

She ran.

Fifteen feet across the parking lot. Twenty. Her boots slapping wet asphalt, the tree line getting closer, and for a moment the math worked. She was small and fast and they were big and one of them was holding his face and the other was favoring his knee and Voss was still by the car and the trees were right there—

The knife hit her thigh from behind.

Not thrown. She didn't see it leave Voss's hand. Just the impact, cold and precise, and then her leg stopped being a leg. She went down hard. Asphalt against her palms, her cheek, the side of her head. Gravel embedding in her skin. Blood soaking through her jeans, warm and fast.

She tried to get up. Her thigh buckled. She caught herself on her hands and tried again.

The first real blow came from behind. A boot between her shoulder blades that drove her flat against the ground and emptied her lungs. The second was a fist to the side of her head. Stars. Then a boot to her ribs that made something shift inside her in a way that things aren't supposed to shift.

She curled. Instinct. Protecting her head, her stomach.

They pulled her arms away. Held her flat. Voss's men knew how to pin someone without killing them. The kind of skill that came from doing this enough times that the body mechanics were automatic.

Voss crouched beside her. She could see his shoes. Polished, but worn. The left one scuffed at the toe where the limp dragged it.

"You're protecting someone." His voice was conversational. Like they were back in the car. "Someone who marked you as useful. Someone who's going to try to use you against me."

Anne spat blood. "Nobody's using me."

His fist hit her jaw. Not the theatrical swing of a man proving a point. A short, efficient strike that cracked something in the joint and made her vision white out for a full second.

"Can't have that," he said.

Another blow. Her cheekbone. She felt the skin split.

She tried to bite the hand that was holding her head. Got close enough that he pulled back, and in the gap she twisted and drove her forehead into the bridge of his nose.

Blood. His. For one second, his blood on her face instead of hers.

Then his men had her again. Tighter. And Voss stood up, wiping his nose with the back of his hand, and looked at the blood with an expression that wasn't anger but something worse. Irritation. The mild frustration of a man whose task was taking longer than it should.

He kicked her in the ribs. Once. Twice. The second time she heard the crack, felt the rib go, felt the rasp in her breath change from effort to damage.

"This one's for screwing up my plans," he said.

He hit her again. Jaw. The crack was louder this time. Something in the joint broke or dislocated and her mouth stopped closing properly. She could taste blood and something sharper, a tooth maybe, or a piece of one.

She tried to speak. Couldn't. The jaw wasn't working right.

Voss reached into his jacket and withdrew the thermecine injector. He held it up where she could see it. The cylinder catching the gray afternoon light, surgical markings along the barrel, the delivery mechanism at the tip designed for precision application. A tool built for a specific purpose by people who understood exactly how much damage they wanted to do.

"This is thermecine," he said. Pedagogical. The tone of a man teaching a lesson. "Continental Authority's favorite tool. Compound reacts with living tissue on contact. Acids and proteins that break down cell structure in a targeted cascade. Applied externally, it burns. Applied to soft tissue, ocular tissue, it does something more permanent. The optic nerve doesn't regenerate. The cornea doesn't heal. What it touches, it destroys. And it takes its time doing it."

One of his men held her head still. The other held her arms. She couldn't move. Couldn't turn away.

"This one's because you disrespected me," Voss said. He positioned the injector above her left eye with the care of a man who'd done this before and took professional pride in placement.

He squeezed.

The world exploded into white fire. Pain beyond the vocabulary she had for pain. The thermecine hitting her eye like molten glass poured into the socket. She screamed. The sound tore out of her without permission, raw and animal, and she could feel the compound working, feel it burning through layers of tissue that were never meant to be exposed to chemistry this aggressive. The heat spreading outward from the contact point, the acids finding pathways through delicate structures, the slow systematic destruction of everything the eye was designed to do.

"This one's because I hate you," he said, and squeezed again.

The second application completed what the first had started. Something fundamental changed in her left eye. The world on that side didn't go dark. It went wrong. Shapes existed but lost their edges. Light existed but lost its source. Like looking through water that would never clear, that would never be anything but clouded and distorted and insufficient for the rest of her life.

They let go of her.

She rolled onto her side. Curled around the pain. Every breath rasped. The rib. The jaw clicking wrong. The thigh bleeding into the gravel. And the eye. The eye burning with a chemical patience that said the thermecine wasn't finished. It would keep working. Hours, maybe. Finishing what it had started, eating through whatever tissue it could reach, the cascade continuing until the compound neutralized or the nerves stopped having anything left to destroy.

Voss stood up. Straightened his jacket. Looked down at her the way you'd look at something on the bottom of your shoe.

"Look at you." Quiet. Almost reflective. "Even now, you want to fight. I can see it." He tilted his head. "Maybe you can't, but I can."

He studied her. The way she was still curled with her fists closed. The way her working eye tracked him through blood and swelling. The way her body hadn't surrendered even though every part of it was broken or breaking.

"Shame." He crouched again. Close enough that she could smell his aftershave and the copper of his own blood from where she'd headbutted him. "Pretty thing like you could have gone far with that body." His eyes moved over her. Clinical. Appraising. The way you'd assess damaged merchandise. "Not so much now."

He stood. Straightened again.

"Too bad that brain of yours got in the way."

He looked up the road. Down the road. A car passed on the highway. Didn't slow.

"Shouldn't have been this way." He was talking to himself now. Or to her. It didn't matter. "A bullet would have been cleaner. Faster." He flexed his hand. The knuckles were swelling. "But you disrespected me. And now I have more damage to control."

He hit her one more time. The jaw again. The broken side. Her vision whited out and came back different, the left eye broadcasting nothing but pain and distortion, the right eye struggling to compensate.

Voss straightened up. Breathing harder than he wanted to be. The exertion showing in his face, the flush, the tremor in his hands worse now. He looked old. He looked tired. He looked like a man who'd been doing this for too long and the work had started costing him more than it used to.

"I'm gettin' too old for this shit."

He turned toward the sedan. His men were already moving. The efficiency of people who'd done this before and knew the timeline: how long they could stay, how long until someone stopped at a rest area and found something they didn't want to find.

Voss paused. Looked back at her. The thing on the ground that used to be a seventeen-year-old courier from Beltmoire.

"Do me a favor." Almost gentle. The way you'd talk to a dog you were putting down. "Die."

He walked three steps. Stopped.

"Best thing for both of us."

The car doors closed. The engine started. The tires moved on gravel, then asphalt, then nothing. The sound of the sedan fading down the highway until it was absorbed by the wind and the trees and the particular silence of a place where nobody was looking.

✧

They left her on the shoulder of a rural highway like something that had fallen off a truck.

The engine sound faded. Then the tires on asphalt. Then nothing but her own breathing, ragged and wet, and the small sounds of a body trying to keep itself running when the person inside it had stopped giving orders.

She was on her back. She knew that from the sky. Gray. Late afternoon, or maybe evening. Hard to tell with one eye swelling shut and the other burning through whatever the thermecine had done to it. The world was wrong on that side. Shapes existed but they'd lost their edges, like looking through water that would never clear.

The road was cold under her. Gravel pressing into her shoulder blades, her palms, the backs of her legs. The knife wound in her thigh had settled into a deep, constant pulse that synced with her heartbeat. Blood on her jeans, cooling. Blood in her mouth from the jaw, from the teeth, from wherever his fists had found bone.

Something rasped when she breathed. Broken, probably. Ribs or something deeper. She didn't have the medical vocabulary and it didn't matter because knowing the word for what was wrong wouldn't make it stop being wrong.

A car passed on the highway. Didn't slow.

Anne stared at the sky with her one working eye and felt the gravel under her and thought about how easy it would be to stay here. Just stop. Let the cold come. Let the gray sky do whatever gray skies did to girls who'd been thrown away on the side of roads nobody used.

The floor feels better than standing.

Lena's voice. Quiet. Not cruel. Just true. The truth of someone who'd found the bottom and discovered it was comfortable down there because comfort was just another word for giving up.

You will care. When you see what it's like. How heavy everything gets.

Anne could feel the weight. Lena was right about that. Everything was heavy. Her legs. Her arms. Her ruined face. The air itself, pressing down on her like the sky had a hand on her chest. The sheer physical mass of continuing to exist when someone had just proven, with fists and chemicals and a knife, that her existence was worthless.

It would be so easy.

Another car. Didn't slow.

Get up.

Not her mother's voice. Not Lena's.

Hers.

Get up. You can't do this.

The same words. The exact same words she'd said on her knees on a bathroom floor in Beltmoire, begging Lena to stand. Begging someone she loved to choose the weight over the floor. And Lena hadn't. Lena had closed her eyes and let go and become the thing the city made of people who stopped fighting it.

Get up.

But her hands wouldn't close. Her leg wouldn't answer. The thigh was a dead frequency, the ribs were static, and her eye was broadcasting nothing but pain on a channel she couldn't shut off. She told her body to move and her body told her it was done listening.

Anne Calder tried to get up.

She couldn't.

The gravel was cold and the sky was gray and the highway was empty and she was seventeen years old and she was going to die here because the system broke Calder women and it had finally broken her.

Lena didn't get up.

Anne didn't either.

○

Something else did.

It started in her hand. The right one. Not a decision. Not courage. Something underneath both of those, something that didn't have a name yet because it was only seconds old. Her fingers closed around the gravel. Not gently. The edges cut into her palm and the pain was specific and bright, and it was different from the other pain because this pain she had chosen.

The world shifted.

Not the road. Not the sky. Something behind her eyes. Like a wire tripping in a circuit, a breaker throwing, current rerouting through pathways that hadn't existed before this moment. The part of her that was Anne, the part that was kind and frightened and had a mother's voice in her head and a sister's ghost on a bathroom floor, that part was still on the ground. Still broken. Still looking at the gray sky with one ruined eye and one that was running out of reasons to stay open.

But something was standing up inside her.

She rolled. The thigh screamed. She didn't care. The ribs did something that should have put her back down. She didn't go.

Hands on the asphalt. Gravel embedding in her palms. She watched her own arms shake and it felt like watching someone else's body, like she'd stepped back from the controls and something leaner and harder had taken the seat.

Knees under her. Then one foot. The road swam. Blood dripped from her jaw and she watched it fall the way you'd watch rain on a window. Distant. Observed.

She stood.

And looked down.

Not literally. Not with her eyes. But something inside the wreckage looked down at what was left of Anne Calder and spoke.

"Took you long enough."

Not out loud. Not exactly. Somewhere between thought and voice, in the space where a person talks to the parts of themselves they can't control. But the tone was different. Harder. The edges on it sharp enough to cut.

"Just a matter of time before you broke. Look at you."

The inventory was clinical. Mechanical. The same way you'd assess a machine that had been run past its tolerances and finally seized. Blood-matted hair. Jaw clicking wrong. The left eye a ruin of heat and swelling and chemical damage that was still doing its work under the skin.

"If you'd been tougher, you wouldn't be down there. If you'd been smarter..."

A pause. The thought catching on something. Not grief. Not pity. Something closer to anger, but colder. The anger of someone discovering they've inherited a mess they didn't make.

"Gods. What did you let him do to our eye?"

Our.

The word hung there. Shared damage. Shared face. Shared body, with two different things living in it now, one on the floor and one standing, and the one standing wasn't going to waste time crying about what the one on the floor had lost.

She touched her own face. Fingers finding the ruin of the left eye. The skin hot and wrong, the tissue underneath responding to pressure with a sensation that had passed through pain into something more like information. Data. The report of damage that was permanent and total and hers. Theirs.

Her hand dropped. Blood on her fingers. She looked at it the way you'd look at a bill you didn't owe but were going to have to pay anyway.

She turned. The highway stretched both directions into nothing. No landmarks. No signs she could read with one good eye in the failing light. Just road and gravel and the gray sky pressing down on a world that didn't care who was standing on it.

She picked the direction that felt like away from where they'd come.

"Take the back seat for a while." Quiet. Almost gentle, if gentle was something this new voice could do. The way you'd talk to someone who'd been hurt so badly they'd stopped being able to help themselves. Not kind. Kind was on the floor with the rest of Anne's things. But not cruel either. Practical. The voice of the one who was going to walk because the other one couldn't.

"I got it from here."

One step. Then another. The road stretching into nothing she recognized. Her body carrying her forward on something that wasn't hope and wasn't anger and wasn't the stubborn refusal she'd inherited from a city that wouldn't die.

Something new. Something that didn't have a name yet.

It would get one.

You see people as they truly are when they think you're beneath them.

Her mother's voice. The last thread. The last thing that was Anne's, passed forward like a tool handed from one worker to the next before the first one clocks out.

She held it.

The gray closed in. The road kept going. The body kept moving.

Anne Calder was in the back seat. Eyes closed. Done.

The thing behind the wheel didn't look back.

NESSA CODA

The Aftermath

Early Winter, 2173

Regional Medical Center - One Week Later

The report was on my desk for three days before I went to see her.

Subject: Anne Calder. Status: Located, alive, hospitalized. Injuries: Severe facial trauma with jaw fractures, partial vision loss (thermecine exposure), rib fractures, deep thigh laceration, multiple contusions. Prognosis: Permanent disability, extended rehabilitation required, psychological evaluation pending.

I read it three times. Each time the words did something different to me. The first read was information. The second was comprehension. The third was the one where I understood that I'd done this. Not Voss. Not Shori. Not the system. Me. I put a seventeen-year-old girl in the path of a man I knew was capable of exactly this, and I let it happen because her silence was convenient.

The hospital room smelled like antiseptic and the particular kind of quiet that exists in places where people are trying not to die. Anne lay in the narrow bed with bandages around her head that did nothing to hide the swelling, the discoloration, the topography of what had been done to her face. The left eye was buried under white gauze. The jaw was wired. She was smaller in that bed than she'd been in the safe house. The building had shrunk her.

When I entered, her remaining eye found me.

Something was wrong.

Not the injuries. I'd expected those. It was the way the eye moved. The hazel-green tracking me from the doorway to the chair with a precision that didn't match a seventeen-year-old trauma victim lying in a hospital bed. There was no fear in it. No confusion. Just assessment. Cold. Fast. The kind of read I'd seen from operatives with decades of fieldwork, not from a kid who'd been running packages in Beltmoire a week ago.

"You," she said. The voice was roughened by intubation and damage. The jaw barely moved when she spoke. But the word carried something I hadn't expected. Not hate. Not grief. Diagnosis.

"Me." I settled into the bedside chair. "How are you feeling?"

Her laugh came out as a broken rasp. She held her chest to control it, the ribs punishing her for the attempt. "Like someone burned my eye with thermecine because I wouldn't tell them what I knew about you."

Direct. No dancing. She knew exactly why this had happened to her and she was choosing to lay it at my feet in the first sentence. That was the girl from the interrogation room. That sharpness was still intact.

"I'm sorry," I said. I meant it more than I'd meant anything in years.

"Sorry doesn't fix my eye." The remaining gaze didn't blink. "Sorry doesn't undo what that bastard did to me."

"No. It doesn't."

We sat in silence. The monitors beeped. The antiseptic smell settled into the back of my throat. I watched her hand on the hospital blanket, the fingers curled loosely, the knuckles still healing from where she'd hit something. Or someone. The medical report mentioned defensive injuries. She'd fought.

"This happened to me because I was protecting you," she said finally.

"Yes."

"And now you're here because you feel guilty."

"Partially." I leaned forward. "But mostly because you survived something that should have broken you completely. And that means something."

"Means I'm too stupid to die."

"Means you have something that can't be trained into people. I've tried. It doesn't work." I studied her face, the ruin and the resilience coexisting in the same broken architecture. "I can't undo what was done to you. I can't give you back what they took. But I can offer you something else."

"What could you possibly offer me?" The edge in her voice was different from the interrogation room. Harder. Thinner. Like a blade that had been ground down to the point where there was almost nothing left of it. "I'm seventeen. I should be worried about boys and grades. Not this."

"The chance to make sure the man who did this to you never does it to anyone else."

Silence. The monitor beeped. Her remaining eye held mine.

"What kind of justice?" Barely above a whisper.

"The kind that starts with revenge."

She was quiet for a long time. I watched her process it. Not the way the girl in the safe house would have processed it, weighing options with the quick instinct of a street courier. This was something else. Slower. More deliberate. The assessment of someone who'd learned to think in longer timelines because the short ones had already been taken from her.

"When do we start?"

I allowed myself a small breath. "In time. First, how about we get to know each other. My name is Vanessa Kaine. My friends call me Nessa. I'd like it if you did the same."

Something shifted in her face. The hard assessment cracked, just slightly, and underneath it was something raw.

"Vanessa Kaine." Flat. Drained. "You could have never showed up. Never checked on me. Let me wonder if you even cared whether I lived." Her hand trembled. "I wish I had died. I wish that bastard had just killed me instead of letting me live like this."

The words hit me like a physical blow because I could see both things at once: the survival mechanism that was running the body, sharp and cold and already calculating how to use what Nessa was offering, and underneath it, buried, the girl. The actual girl. Still in there somewhere. Still hurting in a way the thing running the body couldn't process because it had been built specifically to not process this kind of pain.

"Get out, Nessa. I wish we'd never crossed paths."

I stood. The guilt nailed my feet to the floor, but I forced myself to move. She'd asked me to leave. I would honor that.

I reached down to touch her hand. A farewell. The last contact between us before I walked out and let the system finish what it had started.

Her fingers closed around mine.

Trembling. Not with anger. With fear. The fear of a girl who was alone in a hospital bed with half her vision destroyed and a body that couldn't protect her and a world that had proven, specifically and personally, that it would hurt her and keep going.

Her eye was wet. Her mouth moved. Barely a sound.

"Nessa, please. Don't go."

I sat back down.

I held her hand and watched her cry with one eye, and I understood that I was looking at two people in the same body. One of them had already decided to survive. The other was still on the floor, and she needed someone to sit with her while she figured out whether surviving was worth the cost.

I stayed until she fell asleep.

✡

Same Day | Crestwood Residential, NW Beltmoire
— ❖ —

I returned to the apartment I shared with Shori carrying what I'd seen at the hospital like a stone in my chest. I needed comfort. Shared outrage. Some confirmation that what had been done to a girl who'd protected us was worth grieving.

Shori was reviewing documents at our dining table. Applications and recommendations bearing official seals. Her pen moved with the careful precision of someone doing the most important work of their day.

"I saw her," I said. No preamble. "Anne. The damage is extensive."

Shori glanced up. "I heard the preliminary report. Unfortunate, but not unexpected given Voss's methods. This was anticipated."

"Anticipated." The word sat in my mouth like something rotten. "Shori, they destroyed her eye. Thermecine. Knife wounds. A seventeen-year-old girl who protected us."

"A seventeen-year-old security risk who knew too much about our operations." She returned to her documents. Pen scratching. "Voss handled the situation according to operational necessity."

"You ordered this." Not a question. Confirmation of something I'd been trying not to see. "You told Voss to handle Anne."

Her eyes flicked away. A fracture in the steel. "The ambush required containment. The girl's transfer couldn't be connected to Pence. His political position requires clean hands." Her voice held calculation the way a pipe holds pressure. "I handle what needs handling."

"She was loyal. She chose to protect rather than betray."

"She was a liability who posed a direct threat to everything I've built." Shori looked up. Not regret. Irritation. "Do you understand what's at stake? Chief Minister Pence Garda has been personally reviewing my advancement recommendations. Positions are opening. Continental-level influence. Policy formation, not just implementation."

"Your advancement."

"Our future. The kind of strategic positioning that transcends regional operations." Her excitement was genuine. The most animated I'd seen her in months. "But that requires absolute discretion. Zero security risks. No loose ends."

"Anne wasn't a loose end. She was a person."

"Anne was damaged goods with questionable loyalties and personal grudges." Shori returned to her paperwork. Dismissed. Done. "Voss ensured she won't be identifying anyone or threatening anyone's career trajectory. Problem solved."

The words hung between us.

"I'm going back to see her," I said.

"That's not advisable. Distance yourself from compromised assets."

"I'm not asking for advice. I'm informing you of my decision."

"Nessa." Shori rose. The fluid grace I'd once found compelling. Her voice going soft. Gentle. The voice that had always made me feel safe. "Come here."

She pulled me into her arms. Her hands found my hair, fingers working through the tangles with the same methodical care she brought to everything else. Her other hand traced slow circles on my back. The familiar rhythm. The one that used to mean I was loved.

"Don't let sentiment override strategic thinking," she whispered against my ear. Her breath warm. Intimate. "I've built something important here. Something that could change everything for us." Her arms tightened. Possessive. "Don't compromise it for a pawn that has already been removed from play."

Her hands offering comfort. Her words offering calculation. The gestures of a woman who was soothing me the way you calm a horse that might bolt. Not out of love. Out of control.

I pulled free.

Stood at the door. Looked back at the woman who'd taught me about operational planning and institutional advancement. Who'd apparently learned to see the destruction of a child as an acceptable cost for career progression.

"Maybe," I said, "the problem isn't that Anne served her purpose. Maybe the problem is what we've become when we can call a seventeen-year-old girl a pawn and mean it."

I closed the door. I didn't know it then, but I'd just ended a relationship that had been dying for years. The woman on the other side of that door would become Chief Minister. Would build an empire on the bones of people like Anne. Would spend eighteen years believing that control was the same as protection and efficiency was the same as morality.

And I would spend those same eighteen years building the networks that would eventually bring her down. Starting tonight.

✦

Two Weeks Later | Various Locations, Beltmoire
— ❖ —

Finding Voss required the kind of work that didn't leave traces.

I started with Hull. Not in person. Through the channels we'd built over years of operations that officially didn't exist. A coded message on the frequency he monitored between legitimate dispatches. Three words: *Need a location.*

His reply came within a day. Not the location. Something better. A name. One of his quiet contacts, a woman who ran shipping manifests through the northern docks and owed Hull a debt she'd never be able to repay in paperwork. She knew people who knew people who tracked the movements of men like Voss for their own reasons.

I visited her on a Tuesday. A cramped office above a fish processing plant that smelled like salt and old business. She didn't ask why I wanted to find a Continental Authority operative. She just quoted a price and a timeline.

The price was information. I gave her something about the Andori operations in the southern ports, enough to be useful, not enough to be dangerous. She took it the way she took everything: without expression, filed in a place I'd never find.

The timeline was two weeks.

While I waited, I built.

It started with the guards. Voss kept a security detail. Two men on rotation, hired through the mob channels that ran parallel to the Authority's official infrastructure. They weren't loyal. They were employed. And employed men could be re-employed.

I found the older one through a bar on the waterfront that didn't appear on any city map. Bought him a drink. Listened to him talk about his daughter's school fees and the way the work was wearing him down. Didn't ask him anything about Voss. Just listened. Bought another drink. Left my radio frequency on a napkin.

He called three days later.

The younger one was easier. He owed money to people I knew. A conversation. A debt forgiven. A new obligation created. The arithmetic of leverage.

By the end of the second week, I had Voss's location, his schedule, his security rotation, and the certain knowledge that when the time came, the men paid to protect him would find somewhere else to be.

I didn't think about what I was doing. Not in moral terms. The morality had been settled in a hospital room when a girl grabbed my hand and asked me not to leave. What remained was logistics.

This was what I was good at. Finding the pieces. Moving them into position. Building the architecture that would hold when the weight came down.

I didn't know it yet, but I was building the first version of the networks that would define the next eighteen years of my life. The methods I used to find Voss, the contacts I cultivated, the debts I created and collected, the coded frequencies and safe houses and quiet people who could be trusted to be elsewhere when necessary. All of it would grow. All of it would become the machinery that people would eventually call the Architect's legacy.

It started with a girl in a hospital bed and a man who needed to die.

✷

Three Weeks After the Hospital | Warehouse District, Beltmoire

— ❖ —

The guards stepped aside when I approached. Neutral faces. Professional courtesy. The older one met my eyes for half a second before looking away. The debt honored. The napkin repaid.

"Take a break," I said. "Get coffee. Come back in an hour."

They didn't argue. Smart men.

I waited until their footsteps faded. Then I opened the heavy steel door. The hinges groaned.

Anne came up behind me.

She leaned on a walking cane, her weight favoring the uninjured leg. Three weeks of healing had reduced the swelling in her face, but the white bandage over her left eye remained. Her clothes hung loose on a frame that had lost weight it couldn't afford to lose.

Her remaining eye held something that hadn't been there in the hospital.

Not purpose. That's what I told myself at the time. Looking back, I know it was something else. Something colder than purpose. The operational clarity of a person who'd already decided what they were going to do and was now simply walking toward it.

The warehouse was cold. Concrete floor. High ceiling. The acoustics of an empty industrial space where sound carried too far and whispers were dangerous.

In the center, Lieutenant Marty Voss hung from chains attached to the ceiling beams. His arms above his head at an angle that had become excruciating hours ago. His feet barely touching the floor. Blood dried on his wrists where the shackles had rubbed through skin.

He'd stopped struggling a long time ago.

Anne moved toward him. The cane tapping concrete with each step. Slow. Measured. The pace of someone who wasn't in a hurry because the man in front of her wasn't going anywhere.

I followed.

"Well, well." Voss's voice was hoarse, but the crude authority was still there. Diminished. Like a radio signal weakening but not yet dead. "Look what the cat dragged in. Though I guess it's more accurate to say look what I threw out and left for dead—"

He saw me.

The recognition hit him in stages. First my face. Then the implication. Then the full architecture of what was happening.

"Oh, this is rich." He laughed. It cost him. "So bloody rich. This is who you were protecting?" He looked from me to Anne and back. "This traitorous union trash heap?" He heaved against the chains. "Tell me something, kid. Was it worth the eye?"

I stepped forward. "Who were your buyers, Voss? Who wanted the girl?"

His laugh was bitter. "You think I'm going to give up—"

Anne's cane cracked across his shin. The precision was surgical. She'd found the spot where bone sat closest to skin and she hit it exactly hard enough to fracture without shattering. His scream bounced off the concrete walls.

"Let's try again," I said. "Who were your buyers?"

He spat blood. "Go to hell."

Another crack. The other shin. He doubled over, gasping, his weight dropping onto the chains.

"We have time," Anne said. Her voice was flat. Winter stone. The voice of someone who'd passed through emotion into the clean machinery on the other side.

Three more strikes before he broke.

When the words came, they came fast. The dam giving way. Shori's authorization. The Andori coordination. The side arrangement he'd made with buyers who wanted the girl for their own research. The contingency Anne had disrupted by driving the convoy off-route. The rage that had followed. The rest area. The thermecine. All of it spilling out between gasps, each confession another piece of the architecture I'd suspected but needed to hear confirmed.

Shori had ordered the ambush. Voss had played within it. And Anne had been broken because she'd accidentally ruined both plans by being too good at her job.

I stepped back. Nodded.

Anne's cane tapped the floor as she approached him. Her remaining eye burning with something I couldn't look away from.

She reached up with steady fingers and began unwrapping the bandage.

The white cloth fell away in slow spirals. Layer by layer. Revealing the damage underneath.

Voss went still.

The thermecine had done its work with the patience of good chemistry. The socket wasn't empty. That would have been cleaner. Instead, the tissue had melted and reformed into something wrong. Pink and yellow. Weeping at the edges. The remnant of the eye itself still present, clouded, a mass that might register movement in dense fog but would never see clearly again.

She showed him.

He couldn't look away because looking away would mean acknowledging what he'd done, and men like Voss don't acknowledge. They justify. But the justification wasn't coming. His mouth opened and closed and nothing came out.

"You did this," she said. Clinical.

She held up a small metal cylinder. Identical to the one he'd used three weeks ago. A thermecine injector. She'd brought it from the hospital, or she'd acquired one. I didn't ask. Some questions are better left in the dark.

"Travels through the bloodstream," she said. "Burns everything it touches. Six minutes for it to reach whatever you have for a heart."

She found the jugular. The vein pulsing closest to the surface, the anatomy of vulnerability that she'd learned in three weeks of hospital time spent thinking about exactly this.

"I can see movement through my ruined eye. Dense fog. Cloudy shapes. I'll never read fine print again. Never recognize a face from across a room. Never see a sunset the way I used to."

She pressed the injector against his neck.

"Funny thing is, I can still see you die."

She squeezed.

The thermecine entered his bloodstream with the soft hiss of pressurized delivery. For a moment, nothing happened. Then the chemistry began its work, finding its way through vessels and tissue, the compound doing what it was designed to do. His face changed. The color leaving it. The muscles tightening around his eyes and mouth as the burning started from the inside.

"The throat first," she said, capping the injector. Mechanical. Precise. "Then the chest. Then the cardiac tissue." She stepped back. "I hope you feel every second."

Voss's breathing was already changing. Shorter. Harder. The internal cascade beginning.

She adjusted her grip on the cane. Looked at him one last time.

"You said I could have gone far with that body. You were right." She turned toward the door. "Just not the way you meant."

She walked. Didn't look back. The cane tapping concrete. Measured. Even.

Behind her, Voss began making sounds that suggested the thermecine had found its target.

The door closed behind her with mechanical finality.

I stood in the warehouse and watched him die.

It took longer than six minutes. The sounds he made were the sounds of a body being consumed from the inside by chemistry that didn't care about his rank or his connections or the deals he'd made in dark rooms with serious people. The thermecine worked the way thermecine always worked: patient, thorough, indifferent.

I didn't speak. Didn't comfort. Didn't look away.

When it was over, I stood in the silence and the chemical smell and thought about what I'd just helped build.

She'd walked in as Anne. Damaged. Bandaged. Leaning on a cane.

She'd walked out as something else. The bandage off. The eye exposed. The cane tapping the floor with the rhythm of someone who'd found a pace she could maintain for a very long time.

They would call her Snips. The name would come later, earned in ways I'd rather not describe. And despite every effort I'd make in the years to come to reach the girl I'd first met in that safe house, the girl who'd read a room full of operatives and called them on their lies, the girl who'd helped a grandmother with her bags at a train station because kindness was something she refused to let the world take from her...

Anne would remain in the back seat. Eyes closed. Done.

And the thing behind the wheel would keep driving.

❖

I left the warehouse and walked through Beltmoire in the early dark.

The city creaked around me. Old buildings settling. The elevated rail clicking as it cooled. Street vendors packing up their stalls, the last of the day's commerce folding into canvas bags and wooden crates. Somewhere above me, a violin played through an open window. More heart than skill. A melody that had been old when this city was young.

I thought about Shori. About the papers on her dining table. About the career she was building on a foundation of children and compliance and the belief that institutional advancement justified whatever it cost.

I thought about Voss's buyers. The serious people with serious resources who'd wanted the girl with the amber eyes. The girl who was now in a facility somewhere, being evaluated and processed by people whose job titles required euphemisms. I hadn't saved her. I hadn't even tried. I'd been too busy managing the fallout to remember that at the center of all of this was an eight-year-old child who'd been traded between adults like cargo.

I thought about the northern territories. The reports that had been crossing my desk for months. Unrest. Disappearances. Patterns that looked random until you mapped them and saw the shape underneath. Someone was building something up there. Something that made Shori's operations look like a district office.

And I thought about Anne. About the hand that had grabbed mine in a hospital room. About the sound a cane makes on concrete when the person holding it has already decided who they're going to become.

I had contacts. Hull's network. The shipping manifest woman above the fish plant. The guards who'd been re-employed. The debts I'd created and collected. The beginnings of something.

Not a plan. Not yet. But the materials for one.

The city creaked. The violin played. The night settled over Beltmoire like a hand pressing down on a wound.

I went home. Not to Shori's apartment. Somewhere else. Somewhere that was mine.

And I started making calls.

I, Marked

ABOUT THE AUTHOR

JT Baldwin spent thirty years carrying the world of Blood & Steel before he ever wrote it down. The first sketches lived in notebooks shared with his twin brother — game designs, comic characters, half-built mythologies that never quite let him go. They matured in silence through a career that took him from military service to long-haul trucking across the country, the kind of work that leaves a person alone with their thoughts for ten hours at a time. The characters traveled with him.

The Blood & Steel saga foundation is built on three interlocking series: the Ironforged novels, beginning with *Wilted Crowns*; *The Palisade Journals*, a five-novella collection charting the decades of conspiracy and resistance that shape everything to come; and *Forged in Blood & Steel*, an ongoing collection of short stories from the world. He believes the best stories leave readers with something worth thinking about long after the last page — and that the second read should be richer than the first.

He lives in southeastern Minnesota with his wife, where the world keeps growing and the winters are too damn cold and long.